Threads

of

Fate

What's meant to be, always find its way

Kamalika Bhattacharya

Ukiyoto Publishing

All global publishing rights are held by

Ukiyoto Publishing

Published in 2023

Content Copyright © Kamalika Bhattacharya

ISBN 9789360498719

All rights reserved.
No part of this publication may be reproduced, transmitted, or stored in a retrieval system, in any form by any means, electronic, mechanical, photocopying, recording or otherwise, without the prior permission of the publisher.

The moral rights of the author have been asserted.

This is a work of fiction. Names, characters, businesses, places, events, locales, and incidents are either the products of the author's imagination or used in a fictitious manner. Any resemblance to actual persons, living or dead, or actual events is purely coincidental.

This book is sold subject to the condition that it shall not by way of trade or otherwise, be lent, resold, hired out or otherwise circulated, without the publisher's prior consent, in any form of binding or cover other than that in which it is published.

www.ukiyoto.com

Dedicated to Mom

I would like to express my gratitude to my family for continuing to support me as I complete my task. Mom, I appreciate how you always smooth out the edges of my imperfections. I appreciate you encouraging me to persevere no matter what. Although I mourn you, Dad, I still draw inspiration from you in all of my writing.

Thanks to my "best friends" for lending me a healing hand filled with love and care. My favourite place to vent, rest, recharge, and re-energize my spirit.

They are all beloved people, without whom I couldn't have created various characters and the layers of emotions that they deal with. Last but not least, my mentor, Mike, for guiding me to turn my emotions into words in the most unflinching manner.

Contents

Secret Of The Woods	1
An Autumn Affair	6
Angel In Disguise	10
Mirror Image	16
Lesson Of A Lifetime	21
Outnumbered	29
Timeless Bond	33
Metamorphosis	38
About the Author	*44*

Secret Of The Woods

Sera had always desired a large circle of friends. She had some, but they would often mock her, and she was upset about it. She couldn't do much to draw them in. She was a simple young lady. She couldn't persuade people to befriend her. She was spending her winter vacation in her hometown. She had the opportunity to visit a small village. A small village in which nearly everyone knows who lives where. In contrast to big cities, people are connected by heart rather than mobile phones, software, and apps.

Sera asked her mother if she could go out, and her aunt suggested the girls, "Go to the lake". They were all ecstatic and rushed to get ready. They began at 4 p.m. The sunlit sky was azure. After a half-hour walk, they came to a small patch of forest. Sera was walking down the forest when one of the girls, Binny, reminded her of the stories her grandmother used to tell her.

Sera and her friends were on their way down to see some beautiful birds and peacocks. They were plentiful. Walking through the forest corridors may not be appealing to those who live nearby, but Sera was eager to discover more. Despite the fact that they were village kids who knew their way around the forest patches, they got lost and ended up at an old Bunglow.

The kids had come with the simple expectation of watching birds and talking with their parents and peers. They had not anticipated a nightmare. They couldn't hear anything coming from that bunglow. The area appeared to be deserted. However, there was a typical foul odour in the air. Sera and her gang were alerted as a result. She told them that such a foul odour coming from an abandoned place is unusual, and that now that they are lost in the forest, they should try to find out if anyone lives nearby to help them find their way out.

They could hear some whispers as they tried to learn more about the bunglow. They realised that silence is not as frightening as whispers. They considered entering the facility through the back gate. They couldn't stand the stench as they approached the back gate. The order was too strong, and they discovered gunny bags, some of which had tags with male and female names on them.

Sera and her friends were terrified that they had landed in an unknown and dark place. They couldn't believe what they were seeing. They noticed a few men negotiating, while others were cautiously looking around. They mustered the courage to stay and find out what those people were up to. They remained silent. Her village friends were alarmed to learn that something as terrifying as this existed in the forest's cradle. Because it was winter, the sky became dark and hazy. "Shall we go back?" one of Sera's friends inquired. But the majority of them were curious about what was inside.

The desire to know always leads us in unexpected directions. Similarly, one of her friends discovered a path from the backyard to the bunglow and requested that they accompany her. Sera and her friends entered the backyard by walking through the thorny bushes. While they waited to see what was inside, they got scratches on their skin. Suddenly, a young boy could be seen waiting for someone to come and meet him. He was on the lookout for a kidney for his grandfather. He was pleading with them to make the deal work. It was an organ racket place, and all the men who were there appeared to be predators.

They were requesting a certain sum of money from the boy. Despite his apparent wealth, he was attempting to bargain for one kidney for his ailing grandfather. Serra and her friends wanted to unearth this hidden hell and bring it to the attention of the police. Two of them made the decision to go to the police station.

They did, and as they were wrapping up, the officer asked those two girls to guide them there. The Sub Inspector went to inform the Superintendent, and they quickly assembled a team to track down this location and bust the racket.

They arrived at the location with the intention of catching them red-handed. As a result, a police officer disguised himself and went into the bunglow to strike a deal with them. He noticed various people waiting for their turn, as if they were dealing with life and death. The officer who went inside was astounded to see how everything was pipelined. There were counters and agents who made large sums of money in exchange for human corpses.

Sera noticed that one of those men was attempting to hit the police officer disguised. She couldn't wait any longer and aimed them with a dart pin she had in her pocket. This heightened the police team's alertness, and they revealed their intent to apprehend all those involved in the racket. They were apprehended by police after a brief brawl. Although the police were aware that Sera and her friends were present, they never summoned them and preferred that they remain undercover because they were minors and could cause them problems in the future.

Sera and her friends decided to return home after the police had sealed the bunglow and left. Sera's mother and grandparents were concerned about her and wanted to scold her for acting irresponsibly by staying out in the forest for such an extended period of time. However, the police sub inspector arrived quickly and explained everything to them; they praised her bravery and wit for uncovering such heinous act.

The inspector also informed her parents that because this is a serious and important case, the children will be rewarded by the government for their foresight. Even though Sera's mother was terrified at first, her eyes welled up as she saw her brave and courageous daughter take all of this in stride. Deep down, she was filled with pride.

An Autumn Affair

The azure blue sky, speckled with white clouds, is making all the difference. It conveys the message that the autumn festival of Dusshera is approaching. The beautiful Kans grass is casting a spell over the fields and looks stunning when it sways in sync with the winds.

Madhu has been looking forward to her Dusshera vacation. It's a time of pure bliss and joy, complete with lights, music, food, and, of course, a few festivities. She went to the market and purchased two new dresses for herself, and her father encouraged her to purchase more. She, on the other hand, denied it. She explained, "I don't want to spend money just to be happy, Baba." This Puja season, I'd rather make a difference.

Madhu's father smiled. He was filled with pride. He has raised a bright and caring young lady. She imagined a small child playing in front of her and came running over to grab her hand with a smile. In front of her eyes, a flash of light appears.

She wasn't dreaming, and it gave her a smirk at the corner of her lips. Madhu was very involved with the puja committee, and they were always looking for people like Madhu to help with their puja as volunteers and members.

The durga puja began after a few days, and the idol was all dressed up and ready for the audience. Madhu started visiting pandals in the afternoon and stayed until late at night. She was having a good time with her friends. Madhu entered a magnificently decorated pandal on the sixth day of Dushera, and a young boy immediately drew her attention. He had resigned himself to sitting alone in one corner. There was no crying or talking; there was only silence. This holiday is typically associated with spending time with family and friends.

Even the poorest of the poor should be encouraged; such efforts are made by puja committees throughout Kolkata. Even if not everyone has the opportunity to enjoy a fine meal these days, eating some street food will charge up people, especially children. As a result, finding a boy sitting so quietly in a corner of the puja pandal was unusual. Madhu was undecided whether to ask or not! But she was intrigued by him. She bought cotton candy and gave it to the boy. He looked at Madhu with blank eyes and nodded his head to refuse her.

Don't feel the guilt, Madhu insisted, just have it. I don't have a place to sleep, the boy explained. Please allow me to sleep in your courtyard. He never looked at the cotton candy with greed, because he had been chased out by his stepfather and all he wanted was to make his own way. Madhu sat next to him and asked him to tell him his story. The boy kept asking her if he could sleep in her courtyard. He stated that he can clean her house and perform all household chores neatly.

At this moment, what he doesn't have is a shelter and that scares him by his core. His half sleeve shirt was dark and shabby. His face had black patches and his body was crying for a bath. Madhu somehow wanted to help that boy. But, she was not sure if her dad would allow this boy in their house. They were not filthy rich nor they were so poor that they can't afford to offer a shelter to a young boy.

She summoned the courage to ask the boy one question: "I can take you to my home and allow you to stay there, but you must follow my words." "Are you going to beat me up?" the boy asked innocently. Madhu was stunned. To respond to his question, her throat became constricted. She avoided further conversation and dialled her father's number. She asked him to please remember that I had told you that I had a wish, and you had said that you would grant it. Today I will ask you a question, and I hope you will not refuse. She then hung up.

She brought the boy home, and his father simply stated, "Ask him to sleep upstairs in the corner room next to the Puja room." Madhu was surprised because she expected her father to question her about bringing this boy home. She was silent and nodded her head as she walked up to the boy and directed him upstairs. "I saw you sitting by him in the puja pandal, I was passing by in the evening," Madhu's father said. When you called, I knew you'd get him home. But I want you to know that "I am proud to have been able to instill such humanity in you." I'm proud that I was able to make you see the suffering of others and take up the charge to make a difference."

Madhu's eyes were smudged with tears, and she couldn't find the right words to respond to her father. "It's Saptami tomorrow, and the festivities have just begun," she explained. Baba, please let me sleep." Her eyes glowed with delight and elation.

The next day, they named the boy "Saptak," and he was welcomed into a family that promised to look after him. Saptak, Madhu said, I don't want you to do housework. I expect you to study. Will you do so? Saptak couldn't believe what he was hearing, saying, "It's been my long-time desire to study, but circumstances and people around me were against it, so I quit and stopped going to school."

They made a memorable Durga puja by accepting Saptak's responsibilities. This appears to be a simple story, but the implications are enormous. Even a single ray of light can break the spell of darkness.

Angel In Disguise

Meena lived in Waynard, a small town. She had a dark skin tone. She was always intimidated by the people who lived around her. Her peers would say things to her that broke her heart. Her father observed everything but never spoke to her. He did, however, always give her a tight hug at the end of the day. Meena went to school one day and was tricked by some students, and she was chastised for something she had not done. She was both hurt and moved. She felt she was not being heard or seen by anyone because everyone was focused on the people's outer skin. They never appreciated her for who she is.

She came home in tears. She continued to sob while preparing the evening meal. There seemed to be no one at home. Her father was yet to return. She kept telling herself that she would tell her father everything she was feeling today. But as soon as she saw her father walk in after a long and exhausting day. She couldn't tell him how she felt. She didn't tell anyone.

She was discouraged. But she was a daughter who understood that her pain would be multiplied by her father's love for her. When she was playing in her house courtyard one day, she noticed a chick and tried to attract its attention and play with her. She took a stick and drew a line, and as she walked on the line, the chick followed. When she saw this, she became excited and brought some red vermilion powder and drew another line with it, which the little chick walked over.

The mother hen was watching the chick play while pecking on the grains scattered around the courtyard. Meanwhile, the chick simply walked over the vermilion line while rolling over it. One of the villagers passing by noticed the chick with vermilion smeared all over it and told the others that Meena is a witch and she is playing a trick on the chick.

As the chick was smeared in vermilion, it began fluttering its wings all over, and as a result, it fell into a water bucket in the courtyard. When Meena took it out and held it in her hand, the vermilion melted and began dripping on the floor. It appeared to be blood-soaked, and a few people who came around to check on her were terrified by it, spreading rumours that Meena is not normal and never allowed their children to speak with her.

This episode was a colossal failure. Meena got herself into this mess unknowingly. There were slanderous rumours floating around about her. It was also difficult for her father to get to work. No one dared to ask him a direct question, but they were gossiping about Meena behind his back. He was deeply hurt, but he had no idea how to shut down so many people at once. When he returned home from work one day, instead of going to his house, he went to the forest. He noticed an apostle over there and sat beside him.

He never bothered him or asked him any questions. He was exhausted and lost in his own thoughts. After a while, the holy man opened his eyes and saw Meena's father, telling him that worry is like a fire that consumes us. Set aside your worries and pray to the almighty, because no one is more powerful than the supreme god. He turned around with tears in his eyes; it's not that the monk declared anything unique, but the positivity he expelled through his words was magical and healing for Meena's father.

He expressed his disdain for his daughter, even when she has done nothing wrong. Everyone accuses her for no apparent reason. This was done solely to humiliate her and force her to acknowledge her flaws. "You must move to a city and try to live a better life," the monk advised. Because negativity will make the child's life miserable." Meena's father regarded him with interest. He asked what if my daughter was subjected to the same torture again because society in the higher realms is more cruel and people judge you based on your appearance, clothes, money, and so on.

The situation was just as bad and desecrating here. He decided to leave to help his daughter recover from her ordeal. He paid Meena to meet the monk back in the forest the next morning before leaving town. She didn't ask any questions, but she did look at the monk with a tear in her eye. "May your hands be filled with healing power whosoever touches you with love and respect," the monk said as he took her hands in his.

May your beauty grow with each healing performed by these hands."

These words gave Meena extraordinary power, and she said, "Please bless me so that I can take care of my father because he has gone through so much pain in raising me." With no fault at his end, the pain and humiliation were paramount. And the holy man said, "Tathastu."

They were on their way to Delhi, the capital city. They found a very small place to live and began to live there. Meena's father helped one person with delivery at his shop. In comparison to his small-town job, he began to earn some good money. People here didn't have time to ask about his family and so on. He was content in one way. The Anganwadi workers invited Meena to join them in making pottery crafts, and she agreed.

One lady burned her hands while working one day, and some women rushed to help her relieve the pain. Meena held her hands and applied ointment with great trepidation, and the lady was relieved of all her pain. She quickly resumes as if nothing had happened to her hands. She blessed Meena, saying, "You have angelic power; may you grow and prosper abundantly." For the first time in her life, she had heard such reassuring words. She felt blessed, and the peace on her face gave her a different glow. She went home and prepared food for her father while waiting for him to tell her about the incident. Her father was astounded to learn of the incident.

Within six months, Meena had transformed into an angel of the poor, and they lavished her with blessings and gifts. Her humility, on the other hand, remained constant. Her modesty was so profound that all the healings she could perform helped her heart heal from all the pain she had previously endured. It was from the inside out. Her face became more serene, and she exuded a different glow.

After a few months, Pradeep, a freelance

photographer who came to the Anganwadi centre to take pictures, noticed Meena quietly working in a corner and photographed her. He was drawn to her angelic features. He took a number of photographs of her without telling her. He returned after observing her for a while. The photos he took were so good that he was recognised by a popular magazine. He was then asked to take more pictures of the girl, which they intended to publish. The photographer was completely overwhelmed. He couldn't tell if it was his photographic abilities or the girl's charm that had brought him success.

He returned to the centre to take more pictures of Meena, but he had slipped and fractured his hairline. Meena was already well-known for her healing abilities. Meena was asked to assist by the Anganwadi head. He was in a lot of pain and couldn't move his body to stand, but Meena's hands made him move and greatly relieved his pain. She asked him to rest and then left for the day. Pradeep was unable to tell Meena about his mission to return to the centre.

When Pradeep recovered, he went to Meena's house and informed her father about the project. Meena's father had no idea what such things could bring money. Pradeep stated that Meena would be paid once the assignment was turned over to the magazine. He apparently agreed because he saw no harm in being clicked for free. He only asked that the photographs not be misused and that his daughter not be embarrassed by any of the clicks. Pradeep assured him that he had committed no such offence.

Meena was photographed, and the images were published in several leading magazines. She was compensated significantly. They eventually moved out of the small apartment and into a nearby apartment. Meena continued to visit the Anganwadi to assist the workers, and they all admired her for her humility.

Her humility was more appealing than her beauty. She was noteworthy not for her outward beauty, but for her inner charm. She accomplished unfathomable success. She received assignments from all over the world, and her wealth multiplied. But one thing she never forgot was where she started. Her journey, her anguish, and her humiliations. She kept her door open to anyone in need of healing. Despite her success, she was unable to reach everyone at random. But she never gave up or became arrogant. Her hand was blessed, and she could see the proud, happy father she had always wanted to see.

Her blessings were numerous.

Mirror Image

There are several ways to see the reflection, one with light and another with a mirror. Sreepur, a small village near Hooghly, was a one-of-a-kind place. People were not supposed to use mirrors in their homes due to old customs. It appears that it brings misfortune to households, and those who attempted to change the customary bear the brunt of their disciplinary actions.

A family of five children lived in Sreepur, with three girls and two boys as siblings. They had lost their parents in an unfortunate incident, and their paternal grandparents were the children's official carers. Although they mourn the loss of their own children, their grandchildren bring them joy and laughter. They were neither too rich nor too poor. They had plenty of farmland and ponds to meet their needs.

The children once planned to go to a fair during the winter. Four of the five siblings went to the fair with their friends and had a great time. One of the sisters noticed a shining item covered in a metal box while they were shopping. They all bought some money to enjoy, and one of them bought that beautiful box, unaware that it contained a mirror. They had never before seen an open mirror. All of the glasses in their home were painted blue and green. They used to look into them to prepare.

They all freshened up after returning from the fair and ate dinner before going to bed. Leena, who purchased the mirror box, never showed it to anyone. She considered telling her grandmother about her purchase of a small mirror box, but she couldn't muster the courage.

She never got a chance to open the box because she was constantly surrounded by her siblings. She stashed it in an old trunk. After a few days, they were all invited to a feast at their neighbours' house. She wanted to check her reflection in the mirror box while she was getting ready. She was always getting compliments on her appearance. So she was curious to see how she would appear in a clear mirror if she could see her own reflection.

She was about to open the trunk when she noticed her grandmother entering her room and stopped herself. While everyone else went to the feast, Leena fretted about not being able to use her latest and most unique purchase. She, on the other hand, didn't want to tell anyone, so she couldn't show her agitation.

They all danced, laughed, and had a good time at the event. Meanwhile, Leena obtained permission from her grandfather and asked him if she could return home once with one of her sisters, promising to return early. Her grandfather agreed. They rushed home, and she took advantage of the opportunity to inspect the silver mirror box. She opened the trunk where she had hidden it, but to her surprise, there was no trace of the box. She wasn't sure if she should raise an alarm about it. She hadn't told anyone about her purchase, and no one knew what she had gotten from the fair.

She decided to remain silent for the time being and returned to their neighbor's house. When she returned, her grandmother asked why she had gone missing, and she could only say that she had gone home because she had forgotten to bring a small gift for her friend.

The next morning, her grandmother learned that a cow and calf had died in their village for unknown reasons. Because it's an unlucky symbol, everyone was upset and scared. The villagers were attempting to determine the cause of the incident. Meanwhile, the villagers received word that the village's goldsmith had been in an accident. This infuriated the villagers. They were all concerned and wanted to know what had caused such a string of unfortunate events.

Leena heard everything and was terrified. She assumed it was because of her purchase of the silver box mirror. Furthermore, because she couldn't find it in her trunk, she was certain that someone had unknowingly opened the box and that this was the cause of all these unfortunate events.

She was so terrified that she didn't eat anything for lunch that day and appeared perplexed and convicted. She was extremely sacred because such unfortunate events would be blamed on her purchase and stupid mistake. She couldn't keep her mouth shut for much longer. She couldn't wait for more calamitous events to occur. She wished to apologise to her grandparents. She went to see her grandmother and discovered her younger sister had a high fever.

They all became preoccupied with taking care of her. Meanwhile, she informed her grandmother that she had something important to tell her. While her grandmother was busy caring for her younger sibling. She approached her grandmother with a pale face and said, "I have something to confess." I had unknowingly purchased a small mirror from the market and had hidden it in our old trunk. But the mirror box is no longer there. We've had a string of unfortunate events since this morning, and I'm sure the mirror box is somehow involved in all of them. She begged her grandmother to forgive her for making such a hasty decision and making an unwanted purchase.

She sobbed a lot and apologised for her actions. While her grandmother listened quietly and hugged her back. She assured her that all of this was purely coincidental and had nothing to do with her purchase. She informed Leena that she had taken the mirror box and had hidden it. "I'm not sure if the legends behind the mirror are true or not," she said. However, a beautiful and tiny girl making a minor purchase cannot be the cause of all the unknown ruins. All of these are myths.

She coaxed Leena, telling her she only wanted her to admit to the purchase. Leena's eyes welled up with tears. Her grandmother had not returned the mirror, but she had made Leena understand that hiding could lead to unwanted and unexpected situations and discomfort. But I never believed in such a legend.

Myths can no longer be translated as they once were in their native land. Only in our own time can we find our meaning. This demonstrates that her grandmother was far ahead of her time in analysing situations and having the ability to solve them with ease. Leena bowed forward to receive her blessings. Because blessings outnumber problems every time.

Lesson Of A Lifetime

Simi excelled in her studies and aspired to a successful career. Despite the fact that she was pursuing her studies with zeal, there was something missing. Her mother always preferred that she be self-sufficient rather than marry. Her mother frequently told her about the accomplishments and goals of other girls. She had always wished for her to become self-sufficient sooner. She wanted her to gain confidence and learn the more difficult aspects of life.

Her father assured her that he would always be there to help her achieve her goals. She intended to enrol in a professional course in order to fulfil her dreams and goals. She prepared for the entrance examination and passed it, gaining admission to one of the country's prestigious institutes. She enrolled in nursing school.

She soon began preparing to leave for her hostel life. Her parents were still having difficulty letting go of her. Despite the fact that they were aware that this was the start of her career and that such separations would occur in the coming days. Parental concern was palpable and unmistakable.

Simi had no idea what was about to happen as she entered a different type of situation. She never had many friends who she would miss, and she was quite focused on the fact that if she wanted to make it big, she needed to make the difficult choices, even if they appeared difficult. Her father continued to prick her with various questions in order to prepare her heart for the difficult voyage ahead. Despite the fact that he was unprepared.

Simi's father made all of the necessary preparations on time, and the day finally arrived when she had to leave, and all the while she was feeling everything she couldn't even think about. Her family's separation letter became a large unexpected wound in her heart, which she accepted because she wanted to fulfil her dreams and make her parents proud of her.

She had previously attempted to do small jobs to supplement her income. Her father, however, never praised her for making such attempts. He had assured her numerous times that she could study whatever she desired; he would simply make the necessary arrangements at any cost. That was a father's unwavering assurance to his daughter. Her eyes would well up when she thought about his deep love.

Her father accompanied her to the campus to drop her off. He wished to see his daughter embark on the career of her dreams. He gathered all of the necessary instructions from the college office and informed her of the rules as well as the things she should avoid. He told her that she should not be afraid to return home. Her heart was racing. She was terrified, nervous, and eager to experience the joy of having been accepted into a prestigious institute.

Simi entered her room. She was assigned room 205. She noticed that the room was already occupied by one person because she had kept her belongings very neatly. She smiled and said, "Hello!!" Swapna was her name. She was originally from Vizag. Simi never asked her many questions at first. She always pays close attention to people before succumbing to their demands.

She never shares her feelings with everyone. She never expresses her outrage to anyone. She smiled at everyone who approached her and returned their greetings. But she never poured herself out to anyone. She later discovered that Swapna is a married woman who is pursuing her career because she was unable to complete her studies and was married off.

Simi thanked her husband and family for their support and for protecting her dreams. She couldn't find a good fit for her to bond with, but she accepted her as a roommate and was never against her. Swapna was a morning person who went to bed early. Simi was never a morning person, nor did she go to bed early. It was difficult to adjust the timeclock while remaining committed to their engagements.

Simi could never fit in with a large group; she always chose a small group of people who are understanding and honest. By the grace of God, she made a few friends who were kind to her regardless of her persona. She never ruled her friends, but she was always accepting and supportive. Those who understood her were astounded by her ferocity. She never blended in with the crowd or made friends for the sake of it. She was always on the lookout for genuine people. Her criteria for selecting friends were never their social status or financial gain.

Swapna, on the other hand, was a regular girl. She never sat in groups and gossiped. But she wasn't as strong, and she knew that in order to survive in the hostel, she had to be strong or belong to a group of stronger people. She had no choice but to follow them. Simi chose to ignore all kinds of chaotic issues in order to maintain peace. She always preferred peace to fleeting happiness.

She was starving one night and had skipped her meals for various reasons. She was aimlessly walking through the hostel corridors, but she appeared tired. A girl from another wing of the hostel approached her and asked if she was okay. Simi couldn't lie and say she was starving and couldn't eat her dinner.

That girl ran back to her room, got some snacks for her, and told her to eat. She quickly became precious to her because she never questioned anything else. Simi was so tired after eating that she thanked her and asked if she could go back to her room and sleep. The girl returned the wave with a smile. Simi forgot to inquire about her room number. She later discovered that the girl who assisted her was part of a group of physiotherapy students.

She was so gracious that she never came before her again to discuss that incident. Simi had the opportunity to mingle with her while they were planning a picnic at the end of the year and discovered her to be a very generous soul. Simi explained that she is an introvert who has never made friends in this hostel. But she feels at ease discussing anything with her. The vibe they shared was so friendly and spontaneous that others had difficulty determining that they had barely spoken to each other.

Priyanka was her name. According to Simi, "She always wished to be a potential earning member of her family and wanted to help her Dad instead of settling down with a family life." Simi inquired, "which means you don't love anyone!" Priyanka responded, "We may not always get what we deserve, so why repent for what is not ours?" This was mature for her age. Simi was astounded to see how well-organized this girl was, and she admired her even more for who she was.

She, on the other hand, was not emotionally mature and often gets hung up on other people's opinions and takes them personally. Despite the fact that she carefully selects her friends, she has never had to deal with a lot of emotional attacks from close friends. Priyanka, on the other hand, left a lasting impression on Simi. Whenever Simi faced a challenge, she would begin to look at things through the eyes of Priyanka. And she easily overcome many obstacles.

Simi was inspired by Priyanka after they finished their course and parted ways for their internship. She admired her greatly and often wondered if they could be reunited. Simi had been working for a hospital for two years when time passed. She was only planning a trip with her mother. She wanted to take her mother to Varanasi for a short trip. She considered doing it with Priyanka. She was only messaging her and calling her on special occasions like festivals and birthdays.

Simi called her, and when she answered, she said, "If you don't mind, come to Puri." I'd always wanted you to come to my house, but our exam schedules clashed, so it never happened. Now that you've decided to take mum to Varanasi, why not Puri? I will be delighted to host you. Simi was overjoyed when she heard this. Despite what she said, I wanted the four of us to go somewhere. I would be delighted to see you, and Puri is an excellent choice of location. Simi soon planned her trip to Puri, and more than anything, she was excited to meet Priyanka.

Simi and her mother arrived in Puri, and Priyanka met them at the railway station. Simi hugged her tightly at first sight. She smiled and straightened her back. She invited them to her home and told them, "It's not a hotel, but we'd love to host you and Aunty and give you some wonderful memories." Simi later discovered that Priyanka had lost both her father and her younger brother in an accident. And she is the breadwinner in her family.

Instead of pursuing a career of her choice, she has taken her father's job. Priyanka introduced her younger sisters and stated, "One of my younger sisters is getting married in 6 months." Simi and her mother were hosted quite well by Priyanka and her family for three days, and on the day they were about to return, Simi confessed her heart to Priyanka, saying that she had received a proposal from a boy who is already in the services and he wishes to marry her. But she isn't ready yet and isn't sure if she should commit to someone like him.

He almost proposed to her after only two meetings. Simi was conflicted about her feelings for him. She wondered what Priyanka would have done in such a situation. Priyanka advised her to ask him to wait and meet with him again in order to better understand and explore him before committing. Simi smiled, looked at Priyanka, and said, "Thank you." I had the same thought.

Priyanka told her that you had once asked me in hostel if I admired or liked someone. Actually, I had feelings for someone but had to let him go. I know he won't return to me. But, just as I care for my family, I care for his mother and father. His brother does not provide financial assistance, despite the fact that his father has some savings, but I assist them as much as I can.

I never loved him for the sake of being able to live a happy life with him. My love was free of all earthly pleasures. Even though I know he's gone forever, I still love him. I satisfy myself by caring for his parents. It's not easy, but it's also not very difficult. Our hands are frequently empty, but our hearts are overflowing with love. There is no greater joy than selflessly loving back.

Simi's thoughts were revived by this statement, and she was astounded by Priyanka. She was overjoyed to be a friend to someone so unique and kind. Simi returned home with renewed vigour and promised Priyanka that she would always be by her side. Her eyes welled up, but she was relieved that she had made such a good friend.

Outnumbered

Gokul, a simple boy who lived with his grandparents, was courteous and charming. He had the same interests as other kids, such as singing, playing volley ball, trekking, and so on. The colourful birds, on the other hand, captivate his heart. He enjoyed watching birds. He was studying photography with the goal of becoming a wildlife photographer. He never turned down an invitation from a friend to visit their hometown because villages are true gateways to nature and all of its elements.

Gokul was overjoyed when his friend Nirav invited them all to his hometown. Nirav has numerous ancestral properties, many of which bear his name. They had a few bunglows and farm houses scattered throughout Chattisgarh. Nirav, on the other hand, wanted to host his friends because this was his final year of college studies. Gokul was always looking for opportunities to visit small towns and villages. There is a silence that pervades the village roads. And the birds' chirping ensures the flourishing of peace and tranquilly all around. Gokul brought his lenses and cameras to capture the best of nature.

Nirav had invited five of his friends to his hometown, so he had left ahead of time to make arrangements for their stay. It was a four-hour bus ride from their hostel. Gokul was at ease. He could already sense the laid-back vibe that is the signature panache of villages and small townships. In such places, there is a deafening silence. Gokul was taken aback when he discovered some incredible birds flying above the tree tops.

He sent his luggage with his friends as soon as they arrived and decided to go to the forest. He couldn't stop praising the amazing floras he saw on the way to the forests. As he walked through one section of the forest, he came across a camp where a few foreigners were staying and talking about the forests. He discovered they were here for research while speaking with them. They told Gokul about an endangered species of migratory bird that comes to this forest to lay eggs. If he can capture images of such birds, he can sell them to various research labs and make a fortune.

However, the challenge is that they arrive between 4 and 6 a.m. They flee to the forests as soon as the sun rises. There is a body of water within the forest where they can be seen in the early morning. Gokul was overjoyed to learn this. He wanted to capture these birds not only because he enjoys bird watching, but also because he wanted to learn and collaborate with larger organisations so that his hobby could become his profession.

He returned to Nirav's house and enjoyed the dinner and company of his friends, while some talked about their dreams of going abroad and others about cracking the entrance exams to secure their future.

Nirav wore a simple smile and never claimed to be on a quest for greatness. He addressed Nirav's family and friends as a young boy. Despite his simple appearance, many people at Nirav's workplace liked him. Gokul asked Nirav's cousins to take him to the forest early in the morning to capture various birds. They agreed to take him, but Gokul didn't tell them which bird he wanted to capture.

He was fond of black colour. His t-shirts and jeans were mostly black. He wore his black tracksuit and set out early in the morning in the hopes of capturing the birds. He was optimistic that he would be able to get some great shots. But, despite trying for three days in a row, he was unable to. He took his mouthorgan with him on the fourth day because he gets bored easily, and he lost hope of capturing those birds as well. He had a favourite song that his mother would hum, and he knew exactly how to tune it on the mouthpiece.

He whistled and began playing the instrument while hiding behind a large tree to await the arrival of those rainbow-colored birds. Their hypnotic colours had a spellbinding effect on me. Gokul paused his music and photographed them from every angle possible. He didn't miss capturing them as they flew with such grace. He was overjoyed to have successfully captured them. He returned to the hostel the next day and worked on the photos he had taken on his laptop before mailing them to the aforementioned organisation.

Three days later, Gokul received a phone call from an unknown number. Because it did not appear to be a known number, he did not receive the call. He received the call three times but never answered it because his friends and grandparents had always warned him about phone number scams. He then went through his mail and discovered that he had received a letter of thanks from the organisation to which he had mailed those photographs.

In addition, an offer letter to join them as a photographer was attached to the mail from them. He was offered a very impressive salary, which was unheard of for him. He was asked for his bank account number because they needed to send payment for the photographs he had submitted. He was given a sum of Rs 50,000. He received the money and returned home to inform his grandparents.

He was overjoyed and couldn't control his emotions as he placed the money in his grandfather's hand. His grandfather burst out laughing and kissed Gokul on the cheek. He had no idea that such a passion could change Gokul's luck. He blessed him and instructed him to prepare for and seize the opportunity to shape his future.

by Kamalika Bhattacharya

Timeless Bond

When we enter the world of school and see so many different faces, we are all looking for one face that connects with us like no other. We're all looking for that one special friend. Someone we'd feel comfortable confiding in. A person with whom we could communicate and vice versa. In the midst of the chaos, when we don't want to give up but can see our loose ends, all we want is someone who doesn't judge our flaws and accepts us for who we are.

It was a rainy evening; a good shower of rain had splashed across the city, repainted it, and restored some freshness. Preeti finished her housework and took a half-hour break to walk around the apartment lawn. She only had school friends who were with her because she was good at studies and could quickly make study notes for all subjects. This was her fortitude. But she was not well-liked at school for any other reason.

Pratham, a student at her school, used to live near her flat a few lanes away. He had come to Preeti's flat to see someone. He noticed Preeti walking around the lawn and approached her to talk. Preeti was hesitant to talk to Pratham because she had never had a best friend and all of her classmates approached her with an agenda. He, too, was an introvert. But he mustered the courage to speak to her casually and quickly. Pratham inquired about her studies and inquired about school and her classmates.

He was eager to talk further. Preeti as well. However, a few ladies from her flat who were out for an evening stroll began vying for her attention, and Preeti became aware of it. She had no choice but to end her conversation with Pratham. She abruptly said, "Bye," and then said, "I'll talk to you tomorrow."

She kept her word and continued to speak to Pratham at school. Both quickly became good friends. Many people assumed they were dating each other, but they were not. And they were learning so much as a group. After many years, they both laughed with a childlike giggle. Because they were good friends and could open up to each other, it was becoming easier for them to focus on their goal of doing well in school.

After a few days, it was Preeti's birthday, and she invited Pratham to her house for her celebration. She didn't have many friends, but she invited a few girls from her class who were nice to her. Pratham's family was neither wealthy nor impoverished. But they were in a financial bind this month, and his father was unable to save any money, and he had declared at home that he would cut back on unnecessary expenses. A friend's birthday is definitely included in such costs. Pratham was always a considerate teenager. He respected his father's wishes and never asked for money to buy Preeti a birthday present. He kept money in his piggy bank. He took some money from there and went to a nearby shop to purchase a gift. He was unable to select a gift of his choice, but later saw a large doll on sale that fit his budget and purchased it for Preeti.

Pratham went to Preeti's birthday party with trepidation and presented her with his gift. He had seen many people give her expensive gifts and she would accept them with a smile, but when he received this gift from Pratham, she was overjoyed and eager to open it. Since it was not worth showing up for. Pratham insisted on opening the gift after everyone had left.

The birthday party began with a massive cake cutting, followed by some caricature artists painting and instantly gifting the guests their small portraits. The setting was transformed into a fairytale scene, with one person sketching tattoos on the hands of the boys and girls in one corner and a magician performing some quick magic tricks for the guests in the other. The lovely pastel-colored décor added to the magical story. Preeti's father had invited his coworkers, but her mother had only invited a few of her friends. They were having a good time in the nail art section.

Pratham was introduced to all possible guests by Preeti. He became preoccupied with some boys from the flat whose parents had been invited. In the midst of all of this, Preeti became intrigued by Pratham's gift. She approached the gift corner and opened his present. She was overjoyed when his friend gave her a cute doll. But one girl burst out laughing and asked Preeti, "Who gave you that cheap doll?"Such dolls are no longer available in any toy store nowadays. Someone saved a lot of money by giving you this. And she continued to giggle with her other friends while pointing at Preeti. She became discouraged when she noticed that many people were staring at her while she was holding the doll close to her.

Pratham noticed everything and became enraged with Preeti for failing to keep her word. He was quietly walking back to his house when Preeti's father caught up with him. He led him to a corner and asked him why he was leaving the party so quickly.

Pratham expressed his disappointment that his gift was not as expensive as others. "Son, I want to tell you something today, please remember this," Preeti's father said, placing his hand on Prathm's shoulder. Never try to avoid responsibility. Especially if you have given something to someone. Always take responsibility for what you do. Never, ever consider what others will think or say. It is critical to determine whether the item chosen is liked by the person for whom it was purchased.

If that criteria is met, it makes no difference what others say. Never jeopardise your relationships with people you don't even know. Learn to ignore and move on. You should remember that you bought the gift to make Preeti happy, not to make everyone else happy at the party. You might have been disappointed if Preeti didn't like the gift."

His words were invaluable. He hugged him and invited him to dinner before heading home. Pratham developed a deep admiration for Preeti's father as a result of this. He received some practical advice that his father could have easily avoided. He, however, did not. Pratham felt his resentment fade away, and he was enlightened to see things in a new light.

He ate his dinner and told Preeti, "I don't know who gave you what, Preeti, but I got a huge return gift in your party." Preeti was unsure and assumed Pratham would be sad for her. "I am going back home tonight as a very confident and charged up man from your party," Pratham said before she could speak. "And I will be eternally grateful to your father for this. He turned a serious storm into a delightful learning experience for me that I will remember for years."

Metamorphosis

A lovely young lady Ancy was on vacation this summer. Ancy was twelve years old. During her vacation, she was eager to see her grandparents. She was waiting for her mother to reveal the departure date. Every day, she nagged about her friends and their respective travels.

She asked her mother one day if she could call her two closest friends. Anna and James are a couple. Anna was living with her grandmother because her mother worked in a hospital and she had lost her father when she was five years old. She felt obligated because she was the only earning member of her family.

Despite the fact that Anna's grandmother received a pension and they were able to live comfortably. James had no grandparents on either side of his family. They were obviously very close to Ancy's grandparents. They also treated these children well whenever they came to Ancy. They had known these children for a long time and were very attached to them.

However, Ancy's mother was preoccupied with office work and was unable to reschedule the day of travel. She was also assigned a few tasks that kept her completely occupied and prevented her from spending time with her daughter. She immediately approved Ancy's plan to call her friends and asked her to be patient because she is overburdened with work at the moment.

Ancy was a responsible child who understood her mother's hectic schedule, which was preventing their plan from coming to fruition. Meanwhile, she prepared some quick snacks, such as instant french fries, and asked their cook to make sandwiches for her friends. She made a fruit punch for her friends by combining two different flavours of fruit juice.

Anna and James came to spend the day with Ancy and had a great time. They decided to watch a movie, and while watching the movie, Ancy proposed to her friends that she is willing and eager to visit her Grandparents, but her mom is unable to carry out the plan due to her mother's illness. She stated, "This time, I want you to come along, and we can have a good time at my native." I understand that Mom will be unable to join us because she will be extremely busy in the coming days. And we've been looking forward to this holiday for a long time. Why don't we go out and have fun? If you all agree, I will ask Mom to request permission from your parents.

When they were leaving the kid's party, Ancy reminded them to stay prepared for a fun-filled holiday ahead. They were hoping that their parents would not object to the plan. Soon after, Ancy's mother found out about the plan she had proposed to her friends. She was relieved that her daughter was so accommodating. As a token of gratitude, she informed Ancy that she would be driving them to their hometown and then returning. She also promised to go and spend two days with them when they returned. She anticipates that her workload will be reduced by then.

Meanwhile, she spoke with Anna and James's parents to obtain their permission for this vacation. They were relieved because they had known the family for a long time. Ancy called Anna and James and suggested they bring some games because they would have plenty of time to play and have fun in the native.

They were all ecstatic and began preparing for the journey. They packed their clothes, toys, paints, and paper for crafts, among other things. James, despite being a boy, never felt out of place because their friendship was so strong, and the girls never made him feel out of place either. In fact, he could share a lot with them because they could understand his emotions.

However, the weekend was only one day away, and they were planning to leave early Saturday morning. They prepared, said their goodbyes to their families, and began their journey. Ancy's grandparents lived in the small village of Bilashpur. It took 4.5 hours to get there from Mumbai. The kids enjoyed the drive and were counting down the minutes until they arrived in the village.

It felt like a home away from home.

Ancy's grandparents greeted them warmly. Ancy's mother abandoned her children in the care of her parents. The kids were overjoyed because there were so many treats. They returned to their rooms. Anna and Ancy were in one room, and James was in the next. Despite keeping their bags in separate rooms, they asked their grandparents if they could all sleep in the same room.

They got permission, and Ancy's grandparents came along. They all sat down on the floor mattress. While Ancy's grandmother was telling stories, she kept them all engrossed and they all slept soundly.

The next day, Ancy, Anna, and James went for a walk around the village. They witnessed a few kids fighting and were in poor health. They were arguing about a piece of fruit. This worried the kids. They all came back. They were all taken aback after breakfast by the fact that these poor village children were fighting over a fruit, whereas in cities, parents ran after the children to feed them different types of fruits every day. Some children refuse to eat their snacks and return the box, claiming that the food is boring, whereas these children were eager to grab one piece of fruit.

The simple struggle for survival was evident in every corner of the village. Anna proposed that we cannot change their fate by giving them money because we are children with our own limitations. But there is one thing we can do: we can use our time to educate these children and encourage them to attend government schools that provide mid-day meals.

Ancy and James agreed with this proposal, and they were eager to put it into action, so they decided to assign roles and enlisted the help of their milk vendor to gather the children and persuade them to participate in some fun learning sessions.

End Note

There are various encounters wrapped with a phase of hard nights, crying tears wondering why life is so complex and more often WHY ME!!! But we have to pick ourselves countless times to find what is ahead of us. That is life. Life offers uncountable lessons. A few to remember, a few we never wish to look back. Being perfectly imperfect in your own unique way gives us stories that helps us to emerge and twists the impossibilities. These stories are more of human encounters, if you have some interesting encounters and feel free to share with me, please write to komsb23@gmail.com.

Thank You.

About the Author

Kamalika Bhattacharya has authored poems, short stories, and editorials for a number of journals. Her work deftly combines passion, drama, and love. She has years of valuable professional experience and has worked for a variety of media companies. Her urge to travel motivates her to write down her thoughts and develop a range of storylines. She writes with zeal and expresses a wide range of strong emotions in her work.

www.ingramcontent.com/pod-product-compliance
Lightning Source LLC
LaVergne TN
LVHW041638070526
838199LV00052B/3441